Go Home, River

STORY BY JAMES MAGDANZ

ILLUSTRATIONS BY DIANNE WIDOM

ALASKA NORTHWEST BOOKS™
Anchorage • Seattle • Portland

The author and illustrator would like to express their thanks to five-year-old Amos Woods in Kotzebue, Alaska, and Danny Flory in Arizona for patiently serving as models for the paintings of the young boy in the story.

Library of Congress Cataloging-in-Publication Data

Magdanz, James S.
    Go home, river / story by James Magdanz ; illustrations by Dianne Widom.
        p.   cm.
    Summary: In 1875, a young Inupiat boy travels the length of the Kobuk River with his family, from its source in the mountains of northern Alaska to Kotzebue Sound, where they join others for an annual trade fair.
     ISBN 0-88240-476-8
     [1. Inuit—Juvenile fiction. 2. Inuit—Fiction. 3. Eskimos—Fiction.
4. Rivers—Fiction. 5. Alaska—Fiction.]   I. Widom, Dianne, 1941-   ill.
II. Title.
PZ7.M2715Go   1996
[Fic]—dc20   96-5769
                                                        CIP
                                                          AC

Editor: Marlene Blessing
Designer: Constance Bollen

Note: The illustrations in this book are reproduced from octopus ink paintings. Artist Dianne Widom receives her ink from a fisherman and his wife in Seldovia, Alaska. They use octopus for bait when halibut fishing, as well as for meals. They are always sure to save the ink, rather than let it go to waste. Octopus ink is extremely concentrated, and a few drops go a long way.

Alaska Northwest Books™
An imprint of Graphic Arts Center Publishing Company
Editorial office: 2208 NW Market Street, Suite 300, Seattle, WA 98107
Catalog and order dept.: P.O. Box 10306, Portland, OR 97210
800-452-3032

Printed on acid-free paper in Canada

To Sid and Mary Jane, where the stories began.
—J. M.

To my husband, Ivan, who supports me
in everything I do.
—D. W.

When I was young, I lived beside a wild river. The river was always going somewhere, and I never tired of watching it. My mother told me the river began in the mountains to the north and ended in the ocean to the west. But this I had never seen.

One day my father went down to his boat at the edge of the river. I asked him where he was going. "To the mountains in the north and the ocean in the west," he said.

As I always did, I asked if I could go along. Before he always had said, "Not this time." But this time he said, "Yes."

So we packed the boat—Mother, Father, and I—and set off up the river. Our dogs pulled on the towline, while Mother and Father pushed with their poles. With each bend in the river, the mountains grew closer while the river grew smaller.

At the end of the day, we made our camp on a sandbar. We turned our boat upside down to dry in the evening sun. We cooked over a small fire and listened to geese calling from the lakes. We watched the sun slide behind the mountains and fell asleep on the ground. Each night it was the same.

On the fourth day, with mountains all around us, we left the river. My father lifted me onto his back, and we began to climb the side of a mountain, through spruce trees, across blueberry meadows, up steep fields of tumbled rocks, all the way to the edge of the snow high on the mountain.

The mountains around us were bigger than anything I had ever seen. I felt that I, like the river below, had grown very small.

My father put me down in the snow. I scrambled onto the rocks. My feet were wet. My legs were wet. I looked back and saw my footprints filling with water.

"The river begins here," my father said.

My mother placed dried whitefish and seal oil on a flat rock for us. Eating made me thirsty.

"Listen," my father said. I could hear gentle water under the rocks, but I could not see it. Then I found an opening where a small stream trickled down the mountain. My father showed me how to cup my hands and fingers tightly together to drink.

"The river begins here," he said.

A cool wind began to blow. Clouds darkened the sun and suddenly I was cold. Raindrops splashed on the rocks. Clouds rumbled.

"Come," my father said, and he walked swiftly down an old caribou trail. Lightning flashed. A gray curtain of rain moved across the face of the mountain, closer, and then we were in it. Big drops of rain trickled off my father's hair and onto my cheek.

"The river begins here," my father said.

When we reached the river, it was full of melted snow and swollen with rain. I found a hard, green rock in the riverbed, and I showed it to my father. His eyebrows rose.

"Jade," he said. "We can use this." He wrapped it in a caribou skin and tucked it into the boat.

We all climbed into the boat—Father, Mother, dogs, and I—and sped down the rushing river. For five more days, we traveled. Our river met other rivers, and each time our river grew wider and stronger and deeper. It was hard to imagine our river had ever been small.

*T*hen one day, the river began to take itself apart. It split into smaller rivers, first one to the left, and then another, and then again. I asked my father why the river was getting smaller.

My father held out his hand, spreading his fingers wide. "The river ends with many fingers," he said. "This is but one."

*T*he willows drew back from the shore, and then the shore disappeared into the water. All I could see ahead was water and sky, sky and water. The river had become impossibly, fearfully large.

My father could see the question in my eyes. "We have reached the ocean," he said. "The river ends here."

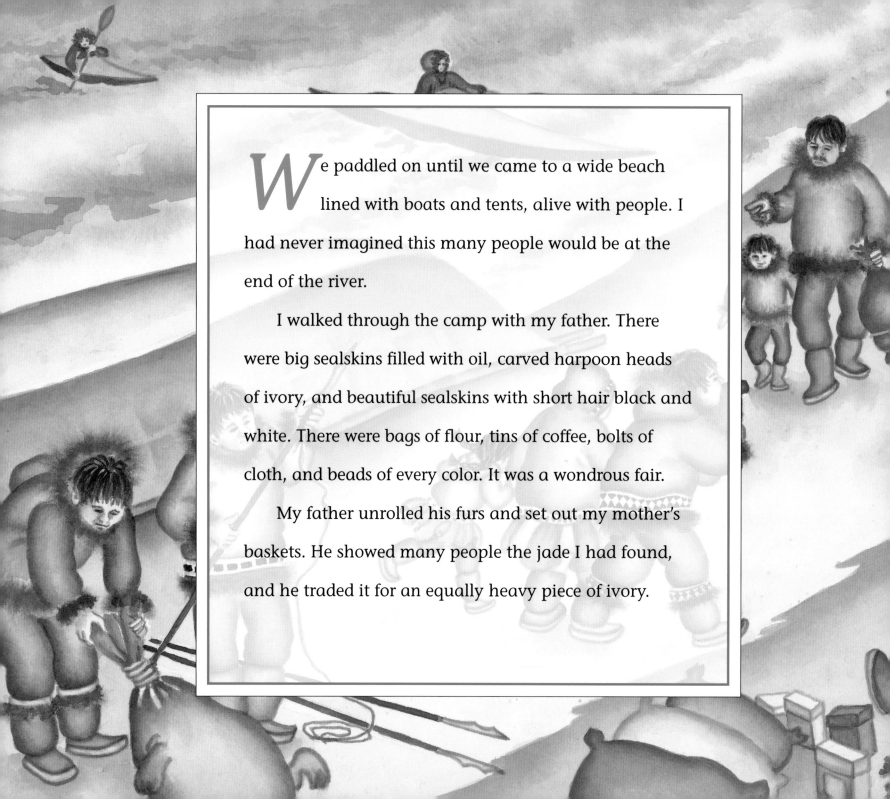

We paddled on until we came to a wide beach lined with boats and tents, alive with people. I had never imagined this many people would be at the end of the river.

I walked through the camp with my father. There were big sealskins filled with oil, carved harpoon heads of ivory, and beautiful sealskins with short hair black and white. There were bags of flour, tins of coffee, bolts of cloth, and beads of every color. It was a wondrous fair.

My father unrolled his furs and set out my mother's baskets. He showed many people the jade I had found, and he traded it for an equally heavy piece of ivory.

*T*he trading lasted for days. Then, one after another, people took down their tents, loaded their boats, and paddled away along the coast.

On the morning we were to leave, a thick fog floated in from the ocean and covered the trading beach. I could hear waves, but I could not see them break on the shore. I could hear gulls argue, but I could not find them in the sky. I could hear people talk, but I could not understand their words. My father came out of our tent. He looked at the fog.

"The river is going home," he said. "The river does not stay in the ocean forever. On cold mornings, it rises into the clouds and goes home to the mountains. When the fog lifts, we will go home too."

*S*oon the fog did lift, and we pushed off from the trading beach

and sailed toward the river. The sun rose higher in the sky and the air

grew warmer.

Far away, the mountains seemed small, but I knew they were not.

I could see snow that one day would melt into the river. I watched clouds

pile into the mountains and lose their rain into the river, too.

We entered the gentle river, and I was glad. I lay down in the boat and felt the river flow beneath me. I could feel each stroke of the paddles pull the boat home. I watched clouds move across the sky. How easy it was for the river to float home in the clouds.

As I drifted toward sleep, I imagined that I, too, was floating home on the clouds. "Go home, river," I whispered. "Go home."

HISTORICAL NOTE

Go Home, River began as a bedtime story for our son. It described a trip we made with him into the Brooks Range in 1992. As I told the story, I wondered how the trip might have occurred in traditional times. It could have been set in many times and places, but I have imagined it occurring about 1875 along the Kobuk River and Kotzebue Sound.

The Inupiat of the Kobuk River contradict many Eskimo stereotypes. They live inland among trees rather than on the coastal tundra, and subsist primarily on fish and caribou rather than on marine mammals. They speak the same language as Inuit throughout the Arctic, but they had unique technologies such as birchbark *qayat*.

In 1875, there would have been as yet no direct contact between Inupiat and Europeans on the upper Kobuk River. Most men and teenage boys spent summer and early fall hunting caribou and sheep in the mountains, while elders, women, and children remained in fish camps.

But a few, like the family in this story, had a life different from their

fellows'. They journeyed every summer to the coast to trade. Long before European and Asian traders arrived in the Arctic, ivory, jade, and fur moved thousands of miles along a network of trade routes. One of the most important trade events in the Arctic occurred each summer at Sisualik, a long gravel spit about ten miles northwest of the modern community of Kotzebue. It was a perfect location: near the mouths of three major rivers, and rich in fish and marine mammals to feed the traders.

The Sisualik trade fair was well known among European explorers, whalers, and traders. One who visited the fair in 1884 estimated that 1,200 people were gathered to watch a single dance. Although the fair's primary purpose was trade, it was a major political and social event. A truce prevailed among warring Inupiat nations, and the warriors' aggression was channeled into intense contests of endurance and skill. The Sisualik fair would have been an exciting place for an Inupiat child in 1875.

—*James Magdanz*